Learning
to
Dance

JESSICA LINCOLN

Revolution

A Division of Inkletting Press

Seattle

ISBN-13: 978-1-950295-00-5

To my readers:
May you all learn to dance

Sitting on the toilet in the midst of my own personal ass Pompeii isn't exactly how I pictured myself when Josh came to pick me up for his family reunion.

I hear his heavy footsteps on our hardwood entry and my stomach buckles.

"Alana?"

"Hold on! I'm coming!" I frantically spray perfume on myself in case I carry any residual fumes with me and then run from the bathroom to grab my bag. I'm an idiot. I know better than to put myself in this kind of situation. Whenever I get nervous my intestines become a breeding ground for the perfect storm, and my angst over a weekend away with my new boyfriend and his family has laid the foundation for a gastric disturbance of epic proportions.

I lug my duffel bag from my room, silently praying to God, Buddha, Allah, or anyone who will listen, that Josh doesn't come upstairs.

"Do you need help with your bag?" He calls from halfway up.

"No! Don't come up!" I screech, not even bothering to mask the panic in my voice. I launch myself and my oversized bag down the stairs, at a speed and velocity that can only mean certain doom. I ram into Josh full speed but he doesn't even flinch. He just looks down at me and smiles, and then effortlessly lifts the bag from my hands.

"Ready?"

"Um, yeah," I summon whatever Zen I haven't left

upstairs in the bathroom or during my flight down, stand on my tiptoes, and give him a kiss. "I just need to stop by the store on our way out of town."

"Oh. Perfect. I need to pick up some sunscreen."

"Oh, I can grab it for you," I say, following him out to his Jeep.

"Naw. I'm not sure which one it is. I need to see the container."

"You sure? I mean, sunscreen's sunscreen. Right?"

"Naw, you've got a sensitive man. I need to be careful or I'll break out."

Wonderful.

"What do you need?" he asks, opening the door for me.

Imodium for my explosive diarrhea. "Um, sunscreen?"

"I knew we were a perfect match." He climbs into the driver's seat and when he looks at me – really looks at me – my insides liquefy even further.

That's the thing about Josh; he sees me.

I have no idea why he chose me. He's cute and funny and smart and I'm... me. Invisible me. Invisibility didn't happen overnight, it was a gradual fading into the shadows until I eventually became the girl people looked straight through. But now that Josh and I are dating, I'm visible once again; a solid person rather than a ghost wandering the hallways of my own high school.

LEARNING TO DANCE

***

When we pull into his grandparents' driveway, we're greeted by trailers and RV's and a lawn pockmarked with tents.

I don't bother to introduce myself, I just head straight to the house in search of the nearest toilet. It doesn't take long to find the bathroom in the little one bedroom cottage. I relax and breathe, thankful the house is empty and everyone is congregating outside rather than in this little yellow cabin with its paper-thin walls.

I flush and pray the plumbing can take it.

My own plumbing feels beyond empty – like my insides have imploded and collapsed in on themselves and then turned inside out. I can't possibly have anything left inside me. Please God, tell me I'm in the clear.

As I'm washing my hands at the pedestal sink, movement catches my eye in the reflection of the mirror. I didn't even notice a second door connecting the bathroom to the bedroom, but it makes sense. A house this small wouldn't have two bathrooms.

In shuffles a woman with long white hair, her skin wrinkled and sagging from sun exposure and mumbling something about a woman named Myrtle. She doesn't acknowledge me, but instead goes directly to the toilet, lifts her flowing skirt, and pees, letting out a trumpeting fart in the process.

I freeze. What do I do? Is she like a T-Rex, where if I don't move, she can't see me? Instinct has me stay frozen, watching the woman behind me in the reflection of the mirror.

We're no more than four feet from each other. I may be used to being invisible, but this is a first. Do I say hi and introduce myself or just pretend like this isn't happening? Before I decide, the woman shuffles back into the bedroom, not even bothering to flush. The moment she's gone I throw open the other door and make my escape to the Jeep where Josh is lifting a tent from the back.

He gives me a mischievous smile. "Our abode," he raises his eyebrows suggestively. "What do you think? Over by the lake?"

"Um, maybe over there?" I point to the corner by the "Port-A-Potty" that's been brought in for the weekend.

"Are you kidding? Way too much traffic. We'll never get any privacy. Come on," he smiles at me. "I've got the perfect spot." He leads me to a little circular patch of grass overlooking the water. Far, far from the bathroom.

***

"So what do you think?" he asks from his seat on the blow-up mattress in the center of our tent. He's taken two sleeping bags and zipped them together to make one giant one. Before I have a chance to answer, he grabs me and pulls me down onto the mattress and kisses me.

My nerves at staying in the same tent together – in the same sleeping bag together – shifts all intestinal activity into high gear.

"Hey Josh!" a pile of pink tulle launches itself into our tent and on top of us. "Mom says you need to help with the burgers."

Austin's a pint-sized mystery; a twelve-year-old tennis prodigy who loves his tutu and his big brother. That's as much as I know. I'm not sure if he's gay or Forest Gumpish or if he's just a boy who likes to wear a tutu with his Converse high tops and AC/DC T-shirts. Josh hasn't offered the information so I haven't asked.

"Hey Alana," Austin says, like we're old friends. "Nonna wants to meet you. She's over by the fire shucking corn with my aunts and my mom. Shuck. Shuck. Shuckers. Shuck you Mother Shuckers." He sings, exiting in the same whirl in which he appeared.

My stomach gives a warning rumble of nervousness from way down deep at the terrifying thought of meeting the rest of Josh's family.

Josh obviously doesn't realize the origin of the rumble.

"Good. I'm glad you're hungry. We're having a Hayward Family Feast tonight – beans, burgers and bratwursts." He gives me another kiss, pulls me to my feet and leads me out to meet the Hayward Clan.

Mother Shucker.

***

"Oh, Alana dear, I'm glad you kids made it safe," Mrs. Hayward says, kissing Josh on the cheek. "Grab some corn and start shucking. Josh, your dad's about to blow up the house again. You should probably go supervise his grilling."

Again?

Josh gives me a kiss on the cheek and runs off to save us

all from a fiery explosion of death, leaving me alone with the Hayward women.

The only seat open is the one right next to the woman from the bathroom, who I can only assume is Josh's Nonna. I can't even bring myself to look directly at her. How much does she know? Did she hear me? Smell me? Or did she even notice I was there? I sit down and a fart is issued forth at record-breaking volume.

But I didn't do it.

"Mother!" Mrs. Hayward scolds the woman, who giggles and pops her dentures at her in response.

"What do you expect? I've been cooking chili all morning. You want the chili, you deal with the consequences. Now, if someone *else* wants to make the chili..."

"Oh Mom, you know none of us ever get it right," Mrs. Hayward responds, laying a hand lovingly on her mother's leg and then turns to me. "Every couple of years we try, but it's just not the same."

A smile hovers on Nonna's lips. She looks down at her corn modestly, her bangle bracelets chiming as she strips the husk off with surprisingly strong hands. I catch Mrs. Hayward's eye and she gives me a barely perceptible wink. I look around at the circle of other women and smiles of conspiracy dance among them.

I've barely shucked my first ear of corn before Austin and his tutu come tearing through our circle, depositing a pile of gold curls and sticky fingers into my lap and singing "here a mother there a shucker everywhere a mother shucker" as he goes.

"Austin, we get it. That's enough!" Mrs. Hayward yells after him, but it's lacking any serious threat to it. My guess is if your little boy's running around in a tutu, you pick your battles carefully.

I look down to find a little girl staring up at me expectantly.

"Chrissy baby, where's your mama?" one of the aunts asks my new lap ornament.

"She and daddy are fighting by the car," Chrissy says, snuggling into my neck and shifting so that her little elbow is poking a critical part of my lower intestines.

"Oh for pity's sake," the woman throws her corn down on the ground and marches off towards the driveway where a group of trailers sit in a half circle. Little Chrissy, with her elbows of death, jumps off my lap and quickly follows.

"At it again huh?" Nonna grins. "They're going to be what keeps this family name going strong. If they're not fighting, they're fu–"

"*Mother*," Mrs. Hayward gently slaps her mother's arm.

"I'm just saying, that girl's trouble."

"That's enough," Mrs. Hayward says firmly.

"What? I'm not supposed to have an opinion when my grandson gets some hussy knocked up? Just try and tell me she didn't poke a hole in that condom herself."

"Mother! Enough!"

"You're not a hussy, are you Alana?" Nonna leans over and whispers loudly to me. My stomach gurgles equally loud in response.

"You know what Mother? I think it's time you checked your chili." Mrs. Hayward grabs the old woman's arm and leads her towards the house.

"Um, I need to use the restroom," I tell the remaining aunt, thinking I'm excusing myself to the outhouse.

"Use ours," she says, pointing to the motor home a mere ten feet behind her.

"Oh, no. That's okay," I say, rising to my feet.

"Don't be silly dear. It's much better than that stupid outhouse. I don't know why they got that thing anyway. Half of us have trailers and we're all family, it's not like we can't share," she shakes her ear of corn at me in emphasis.

I look to the outhouse longingly, but when I see how close it is to the men standing around drinking beer and barbequing, the motor home doesn't seem like such a bad option.

Once inside I stare for a moment in utter awe. I've never seen wall-to-wall crochet before. It's quite a sight to behold. Both the captain's seats in front have crocheted covers, the crocheted couch cover has a giant crocheted blanket folded neatly on top, the little table in the eating nook has a crocheted tablecloth, the kitchen towels are crocheted, what I assume to be the toaster is covered in crochet, and even the rug under my feet is a thicker version of what I'm sure is some form of crochet. I look past the bathroom towards the bedroom and on top of the bed is a crocheted comforter with crocheted pillow cases and throw pillows. But it doesn't stop there. On top of the chair covers and the couch cover, and the tablecloth, sit crocheted doilies in accent colors. You could clothe a village with the amount of yarn in this place.

I refocus on the mission at hand, all the while trying to calculate the amount of noise insulation these walls provide. The second I sit, my stomach cramps and what has been brewing for the last forty-five minutes comes spewing forth at full force with the most beastly groaning sound I've ever heard, like some wildebeest mating call. I cough loudly in a feeble attempt to mask the bellowing of my bowels, but it's useless.

My nether regions are raw and burning, and they feel strangely acidic like I've just vomited from the wrong orifice. The pure science of it is baffling. Where can it possibly be coming from? I haven't eaten all day. It's like my body's been stockpiling for the past week, just waiting to betray me.

When I push the little foot lever to flush, very little flushing actually occurs. It's more like a trapdoor where everything's supposed to drop down and magically disappear. But it's not disappearing; it's plastered to the walls of the mini toilet as fecal shrapnel. I look to my left, and there, hanging on the wall, is a crocheted toilet brush. Its pristine condition tells me this will be the inaugural scrub. I begin to scour, but instead of cleaning, it's smearing.

I flush once more to clear the bowl and try to rinse off the scrubber, but my foot slips from the pedal, snapping the porthole closed and trapping the scrubber in sewage purgatory halfway between Salvation and Hell. I panic and pull, and off comes the poop smeared toilet scrubber *cover*. Who covers their toilet scrubber with a frickin' doily? Now what? I can't exactly retrieve the cover now that it's stained army green. So I do the only thing that makes sense to my frenzied and panicked mind; using the scrubber I shove the stupid crocheted cover down into the belly of the beast and I flee the scene of the crime.

When I step out of the motor home, sweating and shaking, the corn shuckers and their supplies have been replaced by Nonna sitting in a rocking chair under the shade of a tree. She gives me a wide mouthed toothless grin and I tentatively return the smile, self consciously tucking my hair behind my ear. I pray to God her hearing is as decrepit as her social graces. She gives no indication that she's heard a thing, she just sits there smiling her goofy toothless grin. I don't even want to know where her dentures are.

I head towards the direction of the most noise, assuming it's where I'll find Josh. It's a pretty safe bet; he's usually the center of attention.

Right now I just need familiarity. I want him to put his arms around me so I can breathe in his scent and be reminded that for some reason, he chose me.

As I pass under one of the trees, I'm ambushed from above. Something hits my head with a hollow thunk. I search the ground for my assailant and sitting in front of me is a black Converse high-top.

"Sorry Alana," comes a voice from Heaven.

"Austin?"

"Yeah."

"Where are you? I can't see you." I look to the branches

overhead but the leaves are too thick. I move around for a better view and catch a glimpse of hot pink tulle about twenty feet higher than I expected to find him. "Uh, Austin, you're pretty high."

"I know," he says, not registering the worry in my voice, but the pride in his is evident.

"Do you know where Josh is?"

"Where else? Wherever there's the most people," the uppermost branches of the tree says to me. It sounds profoundly wise coming from a tree.

"Could you come with me? I don't know anyone here except for you and Josh," I say, trying to give him my best damsel in distress to lure him down to safety.

I hear a rustle from above and watch as the underside of the tutu drops from branch to branch, quickly descending like an acrobat. It doesn't take me long to realize I had no reason to worry. Austin's more at home in a tree than I am on solid ground.

He drops the last five feet and looks past my shoulder with a smile.

"Hi Nonna," he says, giving a little wave.

I turn around and practically kiss Nonna on the lips. She's standing that close to me.

"Hey Monkey Boy. You're getting pretty good with that tree," she says, brushing past me to rustle his hair.

"Did you see how high I was?"

"I was watching the whole time," she says, flashing her all-gum smile. "But don't you dare let your mother catch you up there. She'll take a chainsaw to that tree herself."

I catch Nonna's eye and glimpse that same sparkle I fell in love with in Josh's. For a second I think maybe she sees me too; like Josh does.

"Edna! Damn it!"

Nonna giggles and shuffles past us towards the group of people congregating around a row of picnic tables shoved together. Austin and I silently follow.

"Oh my, did I hear someone call my name?"

"Edna, if I find your dentures in my drink one more time, so help me God!" Josh's dad hollers.

"So that's where those things ran off to," she mumbles before fishing them from Mr. Hayward's drink and popping them back into place.

"Why, in the name of all that's holy, can you not just keep those damn things in your mouth? You don't take them out, you don't lose them. It's very simple."

Instead of answering him she shuffles off towards the kitchen.

"Paul," she calls over her shoulder, "I'm going to need some help carrying the chili out in a minute."

"Diane, I'm sick of it. It's disgusting."

"I know Paul, I know. She's old." But Mrs. Hayward's

soothing tone isn't working.

"Fine. But why does it always have to be *my* glass? And last Christmas? My mashed potatoes? I'm telling you Diane, the woman's out to get me."

I hear Mrs. Hayward mumble something to her husband.

"No, I'm not paranoid!" he yells indignantly.

Just when it starts getting good, Josh comes up and wraps his arms around me.

"Where've you been, beautiful?"

"Just hanging out with the cute brother," I say, giving Austin a wink.

He beams.

"Thanks a lot Austin, moving in on my woman already?"

"*Your woman*?" I raise an eyebrow.

"Oh, no. We've got a feminist over here!" a hairy beast of a man drawls, drunkenly wrapping his sausage of an arm around Josh's neck. "Don't you know better than to bring one of those around here?"

"Alana, this is my Uncle Hank," Josh says, untangling himself from the bear's death grip.

"Alana, huh? You're parents hippies?"

"What? No."

17

"Good. We can't have no feminist hippies 'round here. This family's a bunch of meat eatin' God fearin' Americans." Hank takes a final swig off his can of Coors Light and crumples it in his hand when the swig proves fruitless.

"Frank, come on over and meet Josh's little girlfriend!"

Hank's mirror image comes sauntering up, a little more stable than Hank, but stumbling none the less.

Good God. There's two of them.

"Frank, this is Alana, Josh's girlfriend. Oh, excuse me," he says laying a calloused hand on my arm, "his special friend – is that what you feminists call yourselves? Or is it partner, like the gays?"

"Girlfriend's fine," I answer quietly, still not sure what to make of Hank.

I reach my hand out to shake Frank's hand, but instead of grabbing a calloused mitt like I expect, I grab something soft and fleshy. Instinct takes over and I scream and jump backwards, wiping my hand off on my jeans and shuddering visibly.

The crowd breaks into hysterical laughter, including Josh.

"Babe, you just made a complete ass of yourself!" he manages to gasp through his wheezy excuse for a laugh.

"FRANK!" Josh's mom abandons her argument with her husband and comes rushing up to hit her brother on the arm. "You did not just do that to the poor girl! What is wrong with you!" she smacks him on the back of the head. Hard.

"Oh, Diane, we was just playin' with her," Frank says, rubbing the back of his head.

"And quit talking like a hick! *You sound like you waz raized in a barn*," Mrs. Hayward drawls in an imitation of them that's spot-on.

"Come on Diane," Hank chimes in, "we was just havin' some fun, right Alana?" He looks at me, but I'm still wiping my hand absentmindedly on my jeans, my eyes searching for what I grabbed.

"Just think of it as a little Hayward Family initiation," Frank says, slapping me on the back and wiggling a raw bratwurst in my face.

"You sixteen?" Hank says, tilting his head.

"Yeah."

"Well, if things don't work out with my nephew, you give me a call in two years," he says wiggling his eyebrows suggestively.

"Inappropriate! In-a-propriate!" Mrs. Hayward hits him repeatedly on the back while Hank giggles and half-heartedly runs away.

"Everyone sit down," Mrs. Hayward yells, obviously fed up with her brothers' antics. "Time to eat!"

We obediently slide into the benches along the tables and suddenly it's a frenzied free-for-all.

"Corn!" Hank/Frank yells from one end of the table.

19

"Incoming!" Frank/Hank yells from the opposite end, lobbing a piece of corn over everyone's heads.

I look to Mrs. Hayward and her lips are pursed tightly, but she doesn't say anything.

I grab a bun, figuring it's the safest option, and load it with slices of cheese. Binders. Please God, make them work.

I'm about to take a bite when my plate is assaulted with a pile of steaming hot diarrhea-inducing chili. My stomach gurgles in fear.

"You've got to try Mama's chili," Josh's aunt says from over my shoulder. "It's legendary."

I pick apart as much of my sandwich as I can, careful to only eat the parts that haven't been infected by the five-alarm gut bomb. The smell alone burns my nose hairs and strips a layer from my retinas. I make sure to push things around on my plate so it looks like I had a healthy serving of Nonna's Famous Chili, although I'm a little surprised it doesn't burn a hole straight through the bottom of my plastic plate.

Just as my stomach begins to feel a bit more settled, the elbows of death climb into my lap.

"Chrissy, where's your mama and daddy?" Mrs. Hayward asks from across the table.

"Having Special Adult Time," she says loudly, producing hysterical laughter from whichever Frank/Hank is closest to me.

"I told you," Nonna calls to her daughter. "All they do is fight and –"

"Mother! Not at the table!"

Chrissy snuggles into my neck once again.

"Chrissy baby," one of the aunts says, "did you get anything to eat?"

She shakes her head.

"What do you want baby?"

There's a lull in conversation while Chrissy contemplates her answer, face still nuzzled into my neck. Then she pulls her head up and proudly announces, her voice broadcasting clear and strong like she has an electric amp attached to her little vocal cords, "When I was little, I didn't need to eat. I used to suck on these," she points to my chest.

Both Frank and Hank hoot like they're going to give themselves a brain aneurism. One of them actually falls backwards out of his seat and doesn't even bother trying to get up. Instead, he rolls on the ground proving to us all just how worthless his belt is, displaying his giant hairy ham hock of an ass with absolutely no sign of shame. My intestines issue a warning clap of thunder. A storm is brewing.

I pray it's not a flash flood.

***

Under the cover of after-dinner chaos, I sneak off for a moment of privacy where I can breathe freely and fart without fear.

I hear Josh calling my name in the distance, but all I want is to be alone. I don't think; I simply run, trying my best

21

to camouflage myself within the shadows of the trees surrounding the campsite. I have no idea where I'm going, I just run. And I run. And I run – straight into Austin.

Actually, I don't run into him so much as I trip over him. What he's doing crouched behind a boulder is beyond me.

"Oh my God Austin, are you alright?"

"I'm fine," he says, holding his hands behind his back in obvious guilt.

"You sure?"

"Fine."

"What are you doing out here?" I give him my best interrogating look and surprisingly enough, he cracks.

"I don't play with dolls," he blurts desperately.

I look down and notice that tucked within his palms is a village of miniature dolls.

I collapse in the dirt next to him. "Good," I say breathlessly. "Neither do I." I smile and pry one of the dolls from his hand. "Hmmm, if I did play with dolls though, this one would be a pretty nice one."

He eyes me warily and then a smile of conspiring creeps across his face. It's not his usual carefree smile he gives as he runs around camp. It's a smile that reaches his eyes and tells me he knows I'm seeing him – and he's seeing me.

I frantically search for conversation. I'm not exactly sure what a twelve-year-old boy does with his dolls, and quite frankly, I'm okay not knowing. "So…" I say, desperately latching on to the first topic that comes to mind. "Nonna seems like quite the handful."

He looks at me and I can tell he's sizing me up with those hazel eyes of his.

"You wanna know a secret?"

"Hmmm?" I raise my eyebrows but try not to look directly at him. I don't want to seem too eager.

"She's faking it."

"Huh?"

"Nonna. She's faking it. It's our special secret. I'm not supposed to tell anyone, but you're different. I know you won't tell."

"Austin, what do you mean she's faking it?" My blood runs cold and my stomach churns. I no longer care about appearing too eager. I need information. Now.

"I mean she fakes being crazy. She says it's her only entertainment since Medicare quit covering Grandpa's Viagra."

"So your grandma…"

"Has perfect hearing – well, with her hearing aids, but she doesn't need them as much as she pretends she does. And she's not crazy. Well, I mean, no more than anyone else."

"Isn't she afraid they'll put her in a home?"

Austin laughs.

"Grandpa'd never let that happen. Besides, he thinks it's funny too. He calls it payback for being teenagers."

My stomach growls a deep warning rumble; further evidence of the impending storm.

Austin looks at me wide eyed. "Nonna promised you wouldn't eat the chilli!"

"I didn't," I answer, my mind reeling even more. She definitely knows. "We should get back. I don't want anyone worrying about where we are."

If I wasn't in dire need of a toilet, I wouldn't be going anywhere near that house right now. She knows. Everything. She hears. SHE HEARS. Oh God, how am I ever going to look that woman in the face?

We return to camp and I slip into the port-a-potty, and bury my head in my hands. Why me? How in the world do I get myself into these situations? I quietly try to release but any sound I make reverberates off the plastic walls of the Port-A-Potty and amplifies every squeak and blow. In the deepest recesses of my entrails there's a wave of movement and the days rumblings culminate in a thunderous evacuation of my insides. I bury my head deeper in my hands, willing myself to just die of embarrassment and get it over with.

I can hear a commotion directly outside the door, but nothing can be done to stop the tsunami. It's inertia, a simple matter of physics; what has been set in motion can't be stopped.

Someone bangs on the door hard enough to dent it, but

all I can do is answer, "Just a minute," in as sing-song a voice as I can muster.

More voices begin to congregate outside and when I realize this mass exodus of my bowels is happening mere feet from whoever's waiting next in line and there's nothing separating us but a plastic door, it makes it even worse.

Another bang on the door, but I can't stem the tide, I just have to go with it.

When the rumbling subsides and the tide recedes, I gather what meager dignity I have left, lift my head high, and open the door to find half the family standing directly outside. They've heard it all.

"Oh Alana dear, I didn't know you were in there! Did Mom's chili get to you too?"

I don't have a chance to answer. Mr. Hayward pushes me out of the way and barrels into the outhouse, letting the door slam behind him. What follows is a louder and more explosive detonation than anything my body could possibly produce.

"Oh God Diane, it burns!" he yells from the interior. "That's it! We're putting that batty old woman in a nursing home!"

"Paul dear, calm down."

"Calm down, that woman tried to kill us all!"

I look past Mrs. Hayward in time to catch a glimpse of the back end of Frank or Hank disappearing into the woods, pants already halfway to his ankles. To my right, Nonna is dancing in the center of the lawn, flinging her bra around her head and grooving to music only she can hear.

She catches me looking at her and gives me a huge toothless smile and then winks. I have no doubt where her dentures are.

Austin comes up beside me and motions for me to lean down. "Stay away from dessert" he whispers before bouncing off to join Nonna in the grass.

"Um, if you'll excuse me Alana, I need to…" but Mrs. Hayward doesn't finish, she's off to the little yellow house at a dead run.

Suddenly, my insides solidify and all my anxiety is gone. Thanks to Nonna, I have nothing to worry about, she's made every single one of Josh's family members human to me. I don't even look to see where Josh is, I just walk over to the middle of the lawn to join a braless Nonna and Austin in their dance. It doesn't matter that there's no music, I have plenty of reason to dance; I'm free… but I'm still keeping my bra on.

Thank you for reading!

If you enjoyed this book, please take a moment to give it a quick review – I promise it won't take long!

If you would like to know when new books come out, opportunities for giveaways, inside information only available to subscribers, contests and so much more, join my online party at:

www.jessicalincoln.com

I promise I will never sell your information (what kind of person does that, anyway).

Or, you can set up alerts and check out my other books on my amazon author page at:

www.amazon.com/author/jessicalincoln

If you want to see what I'm up to or connect with other readers, visit me at:

www.instagram.com/authorjessicalincoln/

or

www.facebook.com/authorjessicalincoln/

Acknowledgments

First and foremost thank you to the Creator of all creativity and to the Bestower of all blessings. I have been truly blessed.

To my loving, faithful and unwaveringly supportive husband. Thank you will never be enough.

To my weekly WAGGERS: this would never have been possible without you. Thank you for your insight, your encouragement and for keeping my brain from turning into mommy mush. Your guidance and critique have made this a better book and me a better writer and your friendship has made me a better person.

To Cindy, Pamela, Tom and Brad: thank you for keeping the houses still standing while we chase those crazy dreams of ours.

ABOUT THE AUTHOR

Jessica Lincoln is an award-winning young adult author. She has been addicted to writing since eighth grade, but never considered writing for a career until she was in college. After earning her journalism degree, she realized she would much rather write about the people in her head than the people on the street, so she quit her job and began writing full time and hasn't looked back since.

She lives in Washington with her husband, two kids and a puppy named Bella. She loves volunteering and celebrating life.

www.ingramcontent.com/pod-product-compliance
Lightning Source LLC
Chambersburg PA
CBHW020144150626
46552CB00021B/1674